The Adventures Of Maggie & Mikey

By William Suchowacki

Illustrated by Megan P. Ericson

Abbott Press books may be ordered through booksellers or by contacting:

Abbott Press
1663 Liberty Drive
Bloomington, IN 47403
www.abbottpress.com
Phone: 1 (866) 697-5310

ISBN: 978-1-4582-1113-2 (sc)
ISBN: 978-1-4582-1112-5 (e)

Print information available on the last page.

Abbott Press rev. date: 01/22/2024

It all began about
five years ago at a
local animal shelter.

This little old couple lost their cat of over 12 years and thought it was time to finally replace him.

As they entered
the animal shelter,
they heard a soft
cry of a pretty black
and white kitty.

The name above the
cage read Maggie.

She was in the
cage scared and
crying because
she was lonely
and wanted a
new home.

So they took her home
and she was still a little
scared because it was
a new place to her.

The little old lady felt so bad that she decided to sleep on the floor with her to help comfort her while she got through her first night.

So the next day came and Maggie felt a little better but they noticed she was still a little scared and lonely.

The old couple thought maybe
Maggie needed a friend and decided
to go back to the animal shelter
to get her a friend to play with.

When the couple came back to the shelter they found another cute little grey kitty with beautiful green eyes.

The cat was cute and friendly
and his name was Mikey.

The old couple
decided to
take him so
Maggie would
have a friend.

When the old couple
came home Maggie
was shocked to
see another cat
in the house.

Maggie and Mikey met and
Maggie was finally happy she
had a friend to play with.

The old couple was happy to see Maggie and Mikey playing together and getting along.

Printed in the United States
by Baker & Taylor Publisher Services